JUN   2006

First Dive
to
Shark Dive

Peter Lourie

Boyds Mills Press

For Suzanna
—P. L.

Before attempting to scuba dive, you should undergo and complete proper training, leading to diver certification.

Published by Boyds Mills Press, Inc.
A Highlights Company
815 Church Street
Honesdale, Pennsylvania 18431

CIP data is available

First edition, 2006
The text of this book is set in 13-point Goudy.

10 9 8 7 6 5 4 3 2 1

The author wishes to thank Tracy Frazier, Harrington (Skeebo) Frazier, Stan Pratt, Tam Stewart, Nick Stewart, and the whole staff at Small Hope Bay Lodge.

Photographs pp. 32, 33, courtesy of the Library of Congress

CONTENTS

Florida

Gulf of
Mexico

Key
West

Florida Keys

Grand Bahama

Red Bays

Nassau

Fresh Creek

Andros

Cuba

Caribbean Sea

Bah

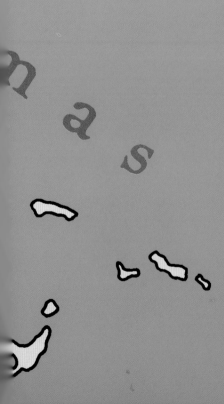

Atlantic
Ocean

PROLOGUE

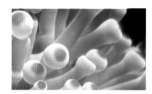

MY DAUGHTER, SUZANNA, WANTED to learn how to scuba-dive. So the week of her twelfth birthday we flew to Andros, the largest, most unexplored island in the Bahamas, a spectacular place for diving.

Flying in a tiny airplane from Fort Lauderdale, Florida, to Fresh Creek, a sparsely populated town on the eastern shore of rugged Andros, Suzanna cast horrified glances at the rough island surface. "Dad," she said, "There aren't any roads down there!"

After flying for ten minutes over the brown wasteland, I spotted a white track in the tropical sunlight. "Look! A road, Suzy!" It was unpaved and without cars. Suzanna scowled. She had hoped for some fancy resort with swimming pools and umbrellas in the drinks.

In fact, we were heading for an extremely modest place called Small Hope Bay Lodge, which had no pool, no drink umbrellas, no phones, and no television. But it was a Mecca for scuba divers. Suzanna would be able to focus all her energy on getting certified as a diver, no small task to accomplish in less than a week. And then, if we had the guts, we could dive with sharks.

DAY ONE
SCUBA INSTRUCTOR

SKEEBO, ONE OF THE LODGE'S Bahamian dive masters, was my daughter's scuba instructor. A wonderful, handsome, and funny man, Skeebo is the son of a Baptist minister. He is humble but extremely competent.

Harrington Frazier (Skeebo is his nickname) had gone on more than five thousand dives at the lodge. Later I learned that when he was twenty-two years old, he had won first place in the 1990 Bahamas Body Building Championships in the junior middleweight division. Now in his thirties, he was just as muscular. What I liked most about the man was his irrepressible sense of humor. His favorite expression,

Suzanna and me

delivered always with a massive grin, was "You better believe it." He said it this way: "You bettah belieeeeeve it," followed with little-boy laughter.

Skeebo's laugh made both Suzanna and me relax a little. Suzanna was nervous about going underwater into an alien world, and I hadn't done any diving in a decade. But what really scared my daughter was the possibility of diving with sharks. At the lodge, she read articles about the subject that both excited and terrified her.

The idea of a shark dive actually frightened both of us because we did not plan to dive with cages; we wanted to swim in the open, with sharks all around us. Long before Suzanna could think seriously about this, however, she had to get PADI certification. PADI stands for Professional Association of Diving Instructors, and it is the world's largest diver-training organization. Skeebo was a PADI instructor. Suzanna would need to become familiar with the diving gear by practicing in a swimming pool, reading and understanding a three-hundred-page diving manual, filling out her medical history and liability forms, taking a written test, and then making four open-water dives with Skeebo. Her first lessons would take place tomorrow in a small pool at a nearby yacht club.

For now, our first few hours on the island, we snorkeled off the beach near our cabin. Suzanna held my hand. We found starfish as big as soccer balls.

BARRIER REEF ON ANDROS

The barrier reef of Andros is the third-largest reef in the world. It extends a distance of 145 miles along the eastern shore of Andros Island. It separates Andros from the Tongue of the Ocean, a 6,000-foot underwater drop-off. The barrier reef is about 1½ miles from shore. Not only is the barrier reef beautiful, it is very sensitive to environmental conditions. The water temperature must remain around 74 degrees for the coral to survive. The entire reef is made up of coral heads and is home to an enormous variety of sea life.

The coast of Andros

THE ISLAND

ONE HUNDRED FORTY MILES LONG and forty miles wide, Andros is mysterious and wild. From 1650 to 1750, the island was considered uninhabited. Only after 1787 was the island settled.

Many of Andros's inhabitants today are descendants of African-born freed slaves from slave ships that passed through Bahamian waters. Perhaps more than on any other island, the people have maintained their African legacy.

*Skeebo discusses the gear (top), and explains what they will
do below the surface (bottom).*

Part of what makes the island so mysterious is the geography. The island is pocked with "blue holes," giant round sinkholes formed in porous limestone and filled with brackish water. These inland blue holes are connected to deep-ocean blue holes miles offshore through a series of twisted caverns and tunnels deep under the sea, where sea devils and mermaids are said to live.

CONFINED-WATER DIVE

THE POOL WE USED FOR SUZANNA'S first dive sat on the edge of the channel into Fresh Creek. Halyards on moored yachts flapped in the stiff wind. Skeebo explained that SCUBA stands for "self-contained underwater breathing apparatus." Then, with his usual you-bettah-belieeeeeve-it good cheer, Skeebo helped Suzanna put on her equipment. A sixteen-year-old local kid named Warren Godette was getting certified at the same time.

Suzanna and Warren would be "buddies." One should always dive with a buddy. A buddy helps put on and check all equipment before a dive. A buddy reminds the diver to keep checking depth and time and air-supply limits while diving. And a buddy also provides emergency assistance, if needed. Having a buddy makes diving more fun—someone to share the experience with.

After Skeebo patiently got both kids outfitted, they stepped into the pool, and down they went. Simple as that. They just slipped below the surface, and I was alone for almost an hour, staring at three dark blotches in the pool, their bubbles rising like soft explosions on the surface.

Skeebo had explained to both kids before they went down that the most important rule of scuba-diving was to keep breathing slowly and steadily. Lungs can be injured by even slight pressure changes if a diver holds his or her breath.

Before they got into the pool, Skeebo had also gone over all the gear in detail, and there's a lot of it.

THE GEAR

ASIDE FROM THE MASK, SNORKEL, AND FINS, there is the *tank*, which holds the pressurized air; the *regulator*, which controls the flow of air to the mouthpiece; and the *BCD*, which is worn like a vest. The BCD, which stands for "buoyancy control device," is an expandable bladder that is

Warren and Suzanna grow more comfortable underwater.

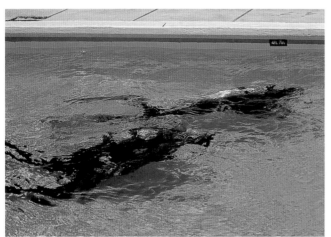

A diver should always dive with a buddy.

11

Masks, fins, and snorkel   BCD

Tanks store high-pressure air for breathing.

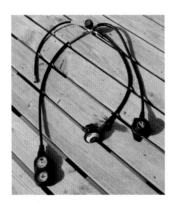

Mouthpiece   Regulator and guages

inflated or deflated to regulate buoyancy. It can be inflated orally, using air from the lungs, or mechanically with the low-pressure inflator, which inflates the BCD with air directly from the tank. To decrease buoyancy, the BCD is deflated through a hose or valve. In addition to a BCD, the diver uses lead weights on a belt as well as lung volume to control buoyancy. Besides allowing the diver to regulate buoyancy underwater, the BCD also provides flotation for swimming, resting, or helping others on the surface.

The scuba tank that is strapped to the BCD vest is a cylindrical metal container used to safely store high-pressure air so that the diver has something to breathe underwater. The valve at the top of the tank controls the flow of air from the tank.

The regulator makes it possible to use the compressed air in the tank. The most important feature of the regulator is that it makes the air easy to breathe. The regulator reduces the scuba tank's high-pressure air in two stages so that it can match the surrounding water pressure. It delivers air only when you inhale, and regulates the air flow. That's how it got its name.

Suzanna, Warren, and Skeebo stayed down a long time, performing lots of exercises. They practiced how to reach what is called *neutral buoyancy*, a way to stay down and not keep popping to the surface. The kids learned how to take off flooded masks, put them back on, and blow out the water. Most importantly, though, this first dive gave Suzanna

Scuba tank regulator connection

BCD oral inflation hose

BCD power inflation button

Lead weight belt

Properly attired scuba diver

and Warren a little self-assurance. I saw my daughter's new-found confidence in her smile when she came out of the water. She beamed when she said, "That was really fun, Dad."

FIRST DAY SUCCESS

SUZANNA'S FIRST DAY had gone extremely well. At dinner, Skeebo whispered, "She's a natural. She just needs to know it." I suppose learning to dive is like learning any skill. Half of what you must learn is self-confidence. Suzanna, however, was still scared of the open ocean, mostly because of the creatures that live there.

After dinner, we walked along the beach near the lodge. Crabs scampered along the sand. I loved this kind of vacation because we had successfully left our electronic devices at home. Our internal clocks were now set to the rising and setting of the sun and the tides. All night we listened to the palm leaves rustling in a stiff sea wind. I had lots of time to read about the Bahamas.

I discovered that the Bahamas consist of eighteen major islands and seven hundred smaller ones, called *cays*. "The amazing thing about the Bahamas," Skeebo said, "is that each island, although so close to the others, is so different. The way we Androsians walk and talk is different than on any other island." In Nassau, the big city on nearby New Providence Island, the minute Skeebo opens his mouth, the people there know he's from Andros and nowhere else.

Goals of the Confined-Water Dive

1. Put on and adjust mask, fins, snorkel, BCD, scuba gear and weights with the assistance of a buddy or instructor.

2. Inflate/deflate BCD at surface using low-pressure inflator.

3. In shallow water, demonstrate proper compressed-air breathing habits, remembering to breathe naturally, and never holding your breath.

4. Clear a regulator while underwater by exhalation and purge-button methods, then resume breathing.

5. Recover a regulator hose from behind the shoulder while underwater.

6. Clear a partially flooded mask while underwater.

7. Swim underwater with scuba equipment while maintaining control of both direction and depth, properly equalizing the ears to accommodate depth changes.

8. Breathe underwater for at least thirty seconds from an alternate air source supplied by another diver (buddy breathing).

9. While underwater, recognize and demonstrate standard hand signals.

10. Demonstrate techniques for a proper ascent: Look up, put hand up, and rotate as you ascend slowly. Always breathe, never hold your breath. If out of air, exhale as you ascend saying, ahhhhh, so that your air is released as your lungs expand.

On her way to becoming a diver

A view of the reef from the cabin

The next morning, I got up early and had coffee. From our cabin on the beach, we looked eastward to a great reef forming a white line in the water along the coast, a giant reef encasing the island, the third-longest offshore reef in the world (after the Great Barrier Reef of Australia and one in Belize).

On the other side of the reef, I learned, there is a wall that drops off precipitously from 90 feet to 6,000 feet, becoming what is called the Tongue of the Ocean. Great pelagic animals, such as sea turtles and whales, rise up from the depths. This is a wonderful place to dive. Out there Skeebo has seen humpback whales and plenty of sharks. No wonder Suzanna was apprehensive.

Also, I read that Andros is like a huge sponge in the sea. The island has an abundance of fresh water. Eight and a half million gallons of fresh water are drawn from the island's wells and shipped to nearby Nassau every day.

When Suzanna woke, she reread the warnings given in the PADI manual. Today would be her first open-water dive.

DAY TWO
BLUE HOLE:
First and Second Open-Water Dives

THE WIND WOULDN'T DIE DOWN. A shallow dive on a coral reef was out of the question. So in the late morning of our third day, Skeebo decided to take Suzanna and Warren to an inland blue hole a few miles from the lodge, where it would be quiet.

Eight full tanks of air rolled around in the back of the crowded van along with our masks, fins, regulators, and a ton of other equipment. These would be Suzanna's first two open-water dives. She had to do four in order to be certified as a diver. On each dive, Skeebo would practice skills that had been introduced in the pool.

A blue hole

A carving of a Chickcharnie

Driving on a dirt road through the pine trees, Skeebo called out, "This is where you find the little houses of the Chickcharnies. I saw one of their houses once, but when I went back to photograph it, it was gone! You bettah belieeeeeve it!"

CHICKCHARNIES

AT BREAKFAST, Skeebo had told Suzanna and me about the legendary creatures that live on Andros, such as sea devils and mermaids. But the most famous was the Chickcharnie. A mythical creature that lives in the pine forests of Andros, the Chickcharnie is said to be half human and half bird, a 3-foot-tall creature with glowing red eyes. It plays tricks on people who do bad things. Skeebo himself saw one when he was sleeping in a hammock. Suddenly his hammock broke. When he fell to the ground, he looked up into the trees and saw two fire-red eyes staring down at him.

Skeebo said Chickcharnies will drop coconuts on your roof at midnight; and if you go out and pick up the right coconut, it will glow phosphorescent green and you will get one wish.

After breakfast, we waited to see if the wind would die down for our open-water dives. Suzanna took the time to study the PADI manual. I was amazed at how determined she was to get certified as a scuba diver. She had yet to make four open-water dives, study the whole three hundred-page manual, and

Suiting up for the blue hole dive

Skeebo carries equipment from the dive shack at the end of the dock.

then take a written test. Skeebo assured her she would do fine, but Suzanna wasn't taking any chances. She studied the manual whenever she got the chance.

While we waited out the wind, Skeebo told me that the half-bird-half-human Chickcharnies protect children until the children are fourteen. Most of the islanders believe this, he said. The creatures know the names of all the boys and girls on the island and even steal into their rooms at night to watch over them. But if a child laughs at one of these creatures or if someone mocks it, Skeebo warned, "She will have bad luck all her life. There will be a permanent spell upon her. You bettah belieeeeeve it! Haaaahaaaa."

In fact, last night one of the dive masters at the lodge had walked out onto the dock and tried to turn on the lights in the dive shack, but the lights wouldn't go on. Suddenly he felt a wind. "Like wings behind me," he told us. Then he heard four steps "like a penguin makes," and then a splash.

Skeebo laughed, "A Chickcharnie, maybe, eh?"

The old logging road to the blue hole was long and bumpy. In these forests, besides Chickcharnies, one can find wild boar. Skeebo told us that some islanders still catch wild boar. If we wanted to, Skeebo said, we could visit a man named Scrap Iron on the other side of the island, in a village called Red Bays. Scrap Iron was an expert at catching wild boar with his bare hands.

Diving in the calm waters of the blue hole

Surgeon fish derive their name from their ability to slash at other fish with their razor-sharp spines.

When we reached the blue hole, Suzanna and Warren put on all their gear at the van and then walked a long rocky path to a cliff facing the round, craterlike hole. It was a 15-foot drop to the water below, which indeed was very blue.

I could tell Suzanna was mightily scared, but she wasn't complaining. Skeebo had told her that if she panicked when she was down deep and raced to the surface, her blood would fill with air bubbles and she could get very sick and maybe even die.

Before she entered the blue hole, Skeebo advised, "Don't put your hands into dark places."

Suzanna worked her way down a rope ladder into the water, where she and Warren began their many exercises. Skeebo made each of them take off their tanks, then put them on again while treading water. Then she and Warren dropped below the surface and practiced underwater navigation with a wrist compass.

Warren got out of the blue hole after two hours of training and said to me with a smile, "Suzanna and I make a great team."

Later that evening, Suzanna wrote in her journal, "*We dove about 25 feet down to practice our new skills. Little fish nipped at our fins and legs. Today was great, but I'm still not sure I have the experience I need for an ocean dive—which is tomorrow! Yikes!*"

At the edge of the blue hole

ADAPTING TO THE UNDERWATER WORLD

THE FIRST THING A DIVER NOTICES is that the world is different underwater — not "normal," yet comfortable and fascinating. A person's senses, which have adapted so well to air and a life lived on land, act differently down there. That's because water is eight hundred times more dense than air. Light and sound and heat act differently below the surface of the water.

Down there, things—fish, divers, coral—look closer

Diving into the blue hole, Suzanna enters another world.

What's a "Squeeze"?

When the external water pressure on parts of your body and equipment is greater than your internal pressure, a painful sensation called a "squeeze" occurs. A squeeze in your lungs can be avoided if you breathe normally and never hold your breath. To avoid a squeeze in the sinuses and ears, and in the mask, a diver must "equalize" on descent.

What's "Equalizing"?

Equalizing is a procedure that brings the external pressure and internal pressure into balance (equalizing usually takes care of itself on ascent). Properly trained divers keep in mind the following tips:

- *Equalize ears and sinuses at the beginning of a descent, and then every few feet thereafter.*

- *Never wait for pain to occur before equalizing.*

- *If you are unable to equalize, ascend a few feet and try again. If you are still unable to equalize, abort your dive. Failure to do so could result in ruptured eardrums.*

- *Equalizing the mask should follow the same timing.*

Ducking behind coral

than they really are. Also, it gets dark quickly as the diver descends. Light from the surface is absorbed by the water. But this absorption is not a uniform process. Different colors are absorbed at different rates at different levels. As white light from the sun (which is all colors mixed) travels down through water it loses certain colors at different depths. First, reds and oranges are absorbed out of the light, then yellows, greens, and finally blues. Deeper water is less colorful, unless you use an underwater light or a strobe on your camera. Without artificial light, everything takes on a uniform brown color.

Sound, too, acts differently in water than in air. It travels about four times faster in water. This makes it hard to know where any given sound is coming from. Sounds seem to come from everywhere.

Corals

Sponges, like this yellow tube sponge, are ancient animals. Fossils of sponges date as far back as 100 million years.

Also, heat is lost at different rates in water. Water conducts heat about twenty times faster than air, so in water, one's precious heat is wicked away from the body quickly. For this reason it is important to wear proper underwater clothing like neoprene wet suits. When the body loses too much heat, *hypothermia*, a condition in which the body reaches a temperature too low to function, can set in. Hypothermia can be a very serious condition, and divers and their buddies should watch out for symptoms of excessive shivering and disorientation.

DAY THREE
THIRD OPEN-WATER DIVE

Sᴜᴢᴀɴɴᴀ Wʀᴏᴛᴇ ɪɴ ʜᴇʀ Jᴏᴜʀɴᴀʟ:

This morning, I studied the manual, then we went diving with Skeebo and Warren and four other people on the dive boat. This time we went to sea. I liked diving with a lot of people because seeing more bodies underwater felt safer.

We went to a little cove around an island. I was nervous, but it was much better than yesterday in the blue hole, which was kind of murky. Here it was super clear. The bottom was sandy with some short seaweed, like a grass lawn, just more spread out. In some spots there was Elkhorn coral.

Skeebo leaned over on his back 20 feet from the surface, and he blew air rings that left his mouth and grew in size as they floated to the sky. He's so relaxed underwater. He picked up a hermit crab, and it came out of its shell and looked at us. I saw two huge starfish. I also saw thousands of black sea urchins. In an old

Elkhorn coral is an important reef-building coral in the Caribbean, providing shelter for many fish and other animals.

CORAL

Corals are not rocks or plants but actually minute animals living together in massive colonies. These animals are called polyps and are only a few millimeters long.

In hard coral, what we see is the outer skeleton of the tiny, fragile polyps. And only the thin, outermost part of coral is alive. The underlying layers are all left-behind skeletons from dead polyps.

Coral reefs are composed of many millions of these polyps. Each polyp builds a case of limestone around itself, using calcium from the water. When these limestone formations increase, they are called a coral reef.

Coral reefs are the largest structures created by any group of animals in the world. They have existed on earth for over 200 million years. They grow in warm, clear, fairly shallow water. The coral cannot grow in polluted water or in water carrying soil from the land.

Organizing equipment on the dive boat

tire, I saw four juvenile striped parrot fish and a bright blue one, also a young parrot fish, I think. I saw small jellyfish, and on the way back to the boat, a huge needlefish (SCARY). I saw a small school of medium-sized snapper.

When I got back to the lodge, just before dinner, I might have seen a Chickcharnie, too. I swear it. Something—it seemed about the size of a toddler—ran by the window so fast, I couldn't see it all that well. When I looked outside, there was nothing there. Dad laughed. Skeebo just said, "You better believe it."

Each night, Dad and I have been walking out onto the dive dock to look for Chickcharnies. Tonight we got to the end of the dock. The moon was out. The breeze blew the palm leaves around. There was a splash off the end of the dock. I held Dad's hand tight. We laughed and shouted, "CHICKCHARNIE!" as we ran for the lodge.

Chickcharnies can swivel their heads around in any direction. Skeebo said they lack a sense of humor. If you cut their pine trees down, they get really angry. The legend about Chickcharnies, I read somewhere, might have originated from real creatures, three-toed burrowing owls that inhabited the forests of Andros before the sixteenth century but are now extinct. Well, maybe not so extinct, eh? Gosh, I love this island!

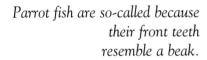

Parrot fish are so-called because their front teeth resemble a beak.

DAY FOUR
FOURTH OPEN-WATER DIVE

THE WIND, THANK GOODNESS, lay down for Suzanna's twelfth birthday. The stillness brought no-see-ums. The sound of doves in the morning was like sweet, sad music. The dogs barking, the roosters screeching, the cars along the road, and the horns—these were all signs of a vibrant island life.

Today was the shallow-reef dive that would be Suzanna's last open-water dive to get her certification. There were lots of divers on the boat.

As we raced out to sea, Suzanna asked Skeebo over the roar of the engines, "Is there a doctor on the island?"

He replied, "Yes, one, but I think he is traveling off island today."

"Only one?"

"You bettah belieeeeeve it," Skeebo said, but instead of laughing, he hugged Suzanna to give her some of his fearlessness.

"I'll be fine," Suzanna said to me, bravely, "as long as I don't see a manta ray, a moray eel, a shark, or a whale."

Skeebo drove the boat to the far side of the reef and

Pork fish (left) and grunts

Suzanna gets her gear ready before a dive.

threw the anchor into the dark blue water. He said, "This place we call Skeebo's Gardens."

Suzanna plunged in with all her gear. Skeebo was right behind her. Today I wasn't diving because I had developed a bad cold with some sinus blockage, which could make descent underwater unbearably painful and dangerous.

I snorkeled over Skeebo and Suzanna, who both looked like fish down there, so relaxed and comfortable. Forty-five minutes later, Suzanna came up, beaming.

Around dinnertime Suzanna took the written PADI test. "She passed," I hooted. Skeebo laughed, "You bettah belieeeeeve it." To him, there had never been any doubt.

Suzanna wrote:

I was stung by jellyfish larva, even through my wetsuit. After Skeebo's Gardens, we dove at another site, called Central Park, near a shipwrecked fishing boat that sticks out above the sea. I dove 25 feet down, saw a ton of great coral and parrot fish. We found a rare burr fish, too; a porcupine fish; and large striped barracuda—scary looking. A barracuda followed me a long distance. I didn't take my eyes off it for fear it might strike, though Skeebo said it never would do that. Later in the day, I got a temporary c-card, they call it. I am certified! I can hardly belieeeeeve it.

The PADI Open Water Diver certification qualifies me to dive independently and get air fills and scuba equipment and other services anywhere in the world. It used to be you had to be twelve to get certified, but recently the rule now is that you can be as young as ten!

Descending into a coral trench

Christmas tree tube worms live on the surface of coral. When they stick their heads out they resemble Christmas trees.

Dad and I walked down the beach and caught a hermit crab. We found coconut shells and broke one open. I tasted my first coconut "flesh." Not bad.

TO SHARK DIVE OR NOT TO SHARK DIVE

I PRACTICALLY DROPPED DEAD at dinner when Skeebo said we could dive with sharks on Friday, if we wanted to. Now that Suzanna was certified and my cold was getting better, nothing stood in our way, except our fear.

Suzanna and I had our doubts. Suzanna had read every shark book and article in the lodge. She was a veritable expert on the subject. Many people, she told me, believe that shark dives, where dive masters actually feed the fish to attract the sharks, might be one reason for the recent spate of shark attacks on the southeastern beaches of the the United States. Others think quite the opposite. They feel that shark dives teach people how to respect sharks. Thousands of sharks are killed every year, intentionally and unintentionally. If we understood them better, maybe we wouldn't kill them.

I realized that no amount of reading on the subject was going to stop Suzanna from diving with those creatures if we had the chance. Suzanna was third on the list for Friday's dive. I had to put my name down after hers. I wasn't about to leave her out there all by herself. Heck, if she was going to get torn limb from limb, I'd better be there. What's a dad for, anyway?

DAY FIVE
HENRY MORGAN

BEFORE FRIDAY, we had some days to explore the island, which allowed us to get to know not just the coral reefs but the people who live on Andros. One of our goals was to dive off Morgan's Bluff. We'd heard that the pirate Henry Morgan had raided ships from the caves up on the bluff, the highest point on the island. Many say he buried his treasure under the water just offshore. But so far no one had found a thing.

Morgan was born in 1635, in Wales. Historians know very little about his early career. In 1670, Captain Morgan led a fleet of pirate ships against the City of Panama, rumored to be the richest city in the world. The city of Panama was a main jumping-off point for Spanish gold on

An artist's depiction of a pirate raid

Skeebo and Suzanna diving on an old wreck

its way to Europe. Morgan sailed into port, burned the city to the ground, and managed to take four hundred thousand pieces of eight, later stealing much of it from his own men.

The first mint in America was established by the Spaniards at Mexico City in 1536, and other mints were set up shortly thereafter in other parts of Mexico and in South America. The coin that was minted in the greatest quantity was a large silver piece with the value of eight reales. This coin soon became the most acceptable trading coin throughout the world. During its history it was given several names: piece of eight, Spanish dollar, and pillar dollar — from the pillars of Hercules, which appear on the reverse side. It is the coin most frequently mentioned in pirate stories and tales of buried treasure.

Throughout his career, Morgan roamed the islands of the Bahamas, allegedly wreaking much havoc and burying plenty of treasure.

Morgan's Bluff, the highest point on Andros Island at 118 feet, is named after him, and it is said that he once hung a lantern there to lure an unsuspecting ship onto the nearby reef, subsequently plundering it after it wrecked.

We wanted to try a search of our own. Skeebo said, "Islanders believe there is a secret cave somewhere. I've been looking all my life, but nothing yet. Let's go have a look. Yes?"

Skeebo drove us north to the bluff. We put on our gear and waded offshore to explore the old wreck. Some people claim the treasure is under the more modern boat that was used for transporting mail and construction materials from

Suzanna getting a closer look at the wreck

Nassau and Florida to Andros.

Although we found not a speck of gold, we had a great afternoon diving on the wreck. Suzanna wanted to swim inside one of the hatches, but I wouldn't let her. We had no flashlights, and I hated the idea of having to rescue her inside if she got lost or stuck in there.

DAY SIX
JOURNEY TO RED BAYS

THE NEXT DAY Skeebo took us to visit his village. Then we planned to head up to Red Bays, the only settlement on the west shore, a fascinating place, where old traditions are still practiced. The people weave beautiful Seminole-style baskets and continue to dive for sponges as islanders did decades ago.

Leaving Fresh Creek for the north, we passed a village called Hopetown, a few cinder-block houses on rugged lime-stone rubble. We stopped in Stanny Creek, as Skeebo calls Stanyard Creek, the place where he was raised. Stanyard Creek is also called the Garden of Andros. Hibiscus grow along the walls of the little church and the schoolyard, and there are flowers everywhere.

Suzanna was amazed at some of Skeebo's stories. When he was little, Skeebo and his father used to go out at night into the

Harvested sponges drying in the sun

SPONGES

Although appearing to be plantlike, sponges are the simplest of multicellular animals. A sponge is a bottom-dwelling creature that attaches itself to something solid in a place where it can find enough food to grow. Called a "filter feeder," a sponge pumps water through its body, capturing and eating particles as small as bacteria.

Most sponges are both male and female. During mating, one sponge plays the male role while the other plays the female role.

Sponges of the tropics come in nearly every color of the rainbow. Sponges take on many shapes, big and small. The barrel sponge can be large enough to put a human inside. Tubular sponges are much, much smaller.

Sponges have an ancient, efficient design that could easily be around for millions of years to come.

mangrove flats, areas of shallow water populated by mangrove trees. They took a flashlight and a machete. Skeebo watched his dad walk in water up to his knees, searching for fish. "On nights when there's no moon, and it's really, really dark, you'll find a big fish just lying there on the bottom. You take your machete and slice the water to hit the fish. But it's tricky—the machete goes wild in water, and you can cut yourself."

Skeebo talked to Suzanna as we drove north of town, where we found large government farming areas: big fields of bananas, beets, corn, tomatoes, cantaloupes, cucumbers, limes, oranges, avocados, apples, and peaches. Farming here is tough work, Skeebo told Suzanna. Bugs or beetles or the weather can destroy everything in a single season. Skeebo shook his head, smiling with a little pain in that smile, remembering the many hours he used to work in his family's fields.

Then Skeebo suddenly launched into a gospel song. Suzanna looked at him and smiled. We had not known he was a singer. And what a beautiful voice he had, too. Apparently, he sings in a choir at the Baptist church in Stanyard Creek, where his father is the minister.

SCRAP IRON

In 1821, Seminoles and black slaves who were escaping persecution in Florida fled to the islands. One of their boats was wrecked off the western shore of Andros, near today's settlement of Red Bays.

"Scrap Iron," from the village of Red Bays

As we drove into Red Bays, Suzanna noticed sponges drying on the ground and fences. Next to a small hut, we met a man named Scrap Iron, also known as Old Goliath, or simply Goliath. He had gray hair and he smiled little. Here was the man who said he caught boar with his bare hands. He made it sound so simple. All you have to do, he said, is come up behind the boar when it's drinking at a pool of water, and "Whap! You hang on. Then you tackle it and cut it with a knife."

Skeebo told Suzanna later that Old Iron is sick and might die. He had eaten an amberjack that had gone bad. Scrap Iron's blood had turned black, Skeebo said. The fish had been six days old, and the dogs that ate some of that rotting amberjack had already died. The flies didn't even want it.

Scrap Iron looked fine to me. Ornery but tough—definitely a survivor. He told us his usual diet was conch, crawfish, beets, okra, cassava, yams, wild pigeon, ducks, and boa constrictors, which grow up to 8 feet long.

BUSH MEDICINE

SUZANNA WANTED TO MEET Miss Marshall, a woman who knew a lot about bush medicine. The people of the Bahamas, and of Andros in particular, have relied for decades on bush medicine when someone gets sick with colds, flu, fevers, coughs, and the like. There is only one doctor on the island, and he lives in Fresh Creek. So

Miss Marshall, an expert in bush medicine

Androsians are trained in the art of bush medicine. Here on the island, medicine is closely tied to supernatural forces, as it has been in West Africa.

Like most children on Andros, Skeebo was trained early in the art of bush medicine.

After talking to Scrap Iron for a half hour, we asked for Miss Marshall, who lived only a few houses away. She was sitting in the dirt among the banana trees, weaving baskets. Around her grew sea grapes, breadfruit, and sapodilla fruit.

She had never been to a doctor, she said proudly. When she or her family got sick, she went to the bush for medicine. Medicinal branches and twigs of this and that species were scattered at her feet. She picked them up one by one to tell us what each plant was good for. Usually the sprigs are made into tea, she said. She would boil sometimes as many as twelve different vines together to make the right potion.

She listed the bush teas. "This one," she said, holding one up, "is for kidney problems." She called it Stinky Pea. "Junivine," she said, "is for strong back." Fire Fingers and Slippery Willey were for more iron in the blood. "This one," she said, lifting another plant, "is for old men, to give them hard backs." Sage was for upset stomach. There were others, too, like "Sweet Margaret," and "Love Vine," which relieve pain. One plant, called "Love Me," was used to determine whether a person truly loves you. If you give the loved one the plant and it turns brown, he or she does not love you.

Bonefish

Bonefishing in the flats

As we drove away, Skeebo told Suzanna it was illegal to take medicine bushes out of the Bahamas. He said he had learned bush medicine from an old lady like Miss Marshall. As a boy he had been much loved by the old people. He said, "I always paid attention to the old folks because I realized they had a lot of useful knowledge."

BONEFISH, "THE GHOST OF THE FLATS"

GAME FISH ABOUND in the waters of the Bahamas, from giant tuna and enormous white and blue marlin to barracuda, amberjack, bonefish, and tarpon. But Andros is mostly known as the bonefish capital of the world.

We met a family of spongers in Red Bays. They had caught a bonefish. It sat on the cooler on their boat, a gleaming piece of silver and gold in harsh midday sunlight. Recently Skeebo had trained as a bonefish guide in the flats, large, shallow, grassy-bottomed areas of the ocean. Bonefish, Skeebo said, have been nicknamed the "ghost of the flats" because of the way they streak like phantoms over the shallows.

On our way back to Small Hope Bay Lodge, talk turned to another kind of sea creature—the Caribbean reef shark, the kind we'd be diving with in the morning. For tomorrow was Friday.

DAY SEVEN
SHARK DIVE

SUZANNA'S WRITINGS ABOUT THE SHARK DIVE capture the excitement, fear, and elation that we both felt:

Sharks. The most misunderstood creatures of the underwater kingdom, and maybe even the entire world. So maybe we are crazy. Today we actually fed the sharks a ball of chum—small frozen fish—so we could get a good look at them.

In the morning I ate a huge breakfast. Then came the news: Skeebo told us the dive was canceled because of the choppy water. Visibility would be way down. I felt relieved, but also disappointed and frustrated. About thirty minutes before we had been scheduled to leave, Skeebo announced the shark dive was back on. He said, "You bettah belieeeeeve it."

Suzanna gets a close look at two Caribbean reef sharks.

Caribbean reef sharks

As our boat sped away from the safety of the land, the butterflies in my stomach multiplied. When we reached the dive site, waves were washing over the boat, almost sweeping away our equipment. Dad lost his dive hood.

No one could spot the buoy marking the place we had to anchor to find the sharks. After searching for fifteen minutes, I'd had enough excitement and wanted to go home. But just then I spotted the buoy. We anchored, but I don't know how. It was so rough.

Skeebo revved the motor, signaling to the sharks that it was feeding time. We were actually summoning them! I slowly put on my gear, feeling nauseated. Dad looked nervous, too, which made me worse. I made him take off his silver wedding ring.

My gear was on. All I had to do now was jump into the wild blue water with those creatures. My stomach plummeted, and I could feel my heart pound.

After hearing a few words of encouragement from the other divers, I gathered some strength. Before I knew it, I was in the water. When my bubbles cleared, the first thing I saw was a shark swimming toward me. I jerked back. Then I remembered that everything seems closer in water than it really is. Small comfort. I wondered if sharks could smell fear.

I counted seven sharks, each averaging 6 feet long. They swam by me slowly, curiously, confidently. Their black eyes were staring into mine.

Finally, Dad came down, and our knees settled onto the sand. We held still, watching the sharks feed on the ball of frozen fish that

Sharks: Bull shark (right), Blacktip reef shark (above the Bull), and a Caribbean reef shark

one of the dive masters secured to an anchor line.

Now there were about seventeen sharks. As I watched them glide and weave through the water, feeding ravenously on the fish, my fear slipped into awe and amazement. I breathed more slowly. These creatures were spectacular. Effortlessly, they moved through the clear aquamarine water, as if slicing it.

One shark was my favorite. I named him "Jaws." He tore off a piece of food, then tried to defend it while the others mauled him for the little scrap of fish dangling from his jaws. "Jaws" would swim away, nothing in his mouth. He seemed interested in us, too. He swam up to our faces — a few feet away, it seemed— then turned like lightning. Could I feel the bubbles coming off his tail?

Once I realized he was not going to eat me, I almost laughed at how scared I'd been. My air was getting low, so I had to swim up to the boat before the rest of the divers.

Sitting on the boat, as we raced away from the magical sharks, I thought it odd that I had been afraid. In the shark-dive argument, I now was firmly in favor of continuing the dive. Sharks are not man-eating, underwater monsters. That's a stereotype. From now on, I will only see sharks as beautiful, elegant creatures to be admired and deeply respected.

GOOD-BYE

BEFORE WE SAID GOOD-BYE, Skeebo drove us to his family land, a cleared area in the limestone rubble. Here he and his wife, Tracy, were planning to build a home and raise a family. Pine forests surrounded the land.

"Chickcharnie country," Skeebo said with that characteristic little boy's smile. "You bettah belieeeeeve it."

Skeebo took Suzanna and me to the tiny airport. Suzanna hugged the man who had taught her to dive, who had taken her out to sea to meet the sharks.

In addition to making a diver of Suzanna and giving her self-confidence, Skeebo had taught us both to love the ocean and the mystery of this wild Caribbean island. Someday soon we planned to come back to search for the sea devils and the mermaids at the blue hole. We'll bring cameras, too, and sit out in the pine forests all night, waiting to catch a rare glimpse of the elusive Androsian Chickcharnie.

INDEX